The Case Of The

HOLLYWOOD WHO-DONE-IT

Look for more great books in

~The New Adventures of~
MARY-KATE & ASHLEY ™

series:

The Case Of The Great Elephant Escape
The Case Of The Summer Camp Caper
The Case Of The Surfing Secret
The Case Of The Green Ghost
The Case Of The Big Scare Mountain Mystery
The Case Of The Slam Dunk Mystery
The Case Of The Rock Star's Secret
The Case Of The Cheerleading Camp Mystery
The Case Of The Flying Phantom
The Case Of The Creepy Castle
The Case Of The Golden Slipper
The Case Of The Flapper 'Napper
The Case Of The High Seas Secret
The Case Of The Logical I Ranch
The Case Of The Dog Camp Mystery
The Case Of The Screaming Scarecrow
The Case Of The Jingle Bell Jinx
The Case Of The Game Show Mystery
The Case Of The Mall Mystery
The Case Of The Weird Science Mystery
The Case Of Camp Crooked Lake
The Case Of The Giggling Ghost
The Case Of The Candy Cane Clue
The Case Of The Hollywood Who-Done-It

and coming soon

The Case Of The Sundae Surprise

The New Adventures of MARY-KATE & ASHLEY™

The Case Of The

HOLLYWOOD WHO-DONE-IT

by Melinda Metz

📽️HarperEntertainment
An Imprint of HarperCollins*Publishers*

A PARACHUTE PRESS BOOK

PARACHUTE
PRESS

Parachute Publishing, L.L.C.
156 Fifth Avenue
New York, NY 10010

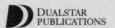
DUALSTAR
PUBLICATIONS

Dualstar Publications
c/o Thorne and Company
A Professional Law Corporation
1801 Century Park East
Los Angeles, CA 90067

HarperEntertainment

An Imprint of HarperCollins*Publishers*
10 East 53rd Street, New York, NY 10022

10 9 8 7 6 5 4 3 2 1

HELLO, HOLLYWOOD!

"Look, Ashley! It's Justin Dare!" I grabbed my twin sister's hand. We were heading into a big Hollywood party in a fancy hotel. And Clue, our basset hound, was with us. She was invited, too.

"I told you Justin would be here!" Ashley cried. She handed me Clue's leash. Then she pulled a camera from her pocket. "Patty's eyes will fall right out of her head when she sees a picture of us with Justin," she said.

Patty O'Leary is one of our friends from

school. Patty didn't believe that we were invited to this party. She wanted proof. And she didn't believe that we could get a picture with our favorite teen actor, Justin Dare.

So that was exactly what we planned to do!

"Justin!" I called out. "Can we take a picture with you?"

Justin turned around.

Ashley gasped. "You're not Justin!"

The teenager looked a lot like Justin. Same height. Same blond hair. Same brown eyes. But Ashley was right. He definitely wasn't Justin Dare.

The boy smiled at Ashley and me. "I'm not Justin. But I *am* the star of *Teen Thief*. My name is Roger Lorre. Do you want my autograph?"

Ashley and I glanced at each other. We had seen *Teen Thief* thirteen times. Roger wasn't in the movie.

"What part did you play?" Ashley asked.

"Brady Calhoun," Roger said.

"But that was Justin Dare!" I said.

"Do you remember the scene where Brady climbed up the side of the Empire State Building with a big sack of stolen coins?" Roger asked.

"Of course," Ashley said. "That was one of the scariest scenes in the movie."

"Well, that was me," Roger said proudly.

A dark-haired man came over to us. "Roger was Justin Dare's stunt double in the movie," he explained. "And I bet I know who you two are. Mary-Kate and Ashley Olsen, the famous Trenchcoat Twins."

"Yup. That's us," I said. "Ashley and I run the Olsen and Olsen Detective Agency from the attic of our house."

"I thought I recognized you!" the man said. "I'm Al Martinez. I sent you the invitation for tonight. Welcome to the Holly awards party." He shook our hands.

"Thanks for inviting us. And for letting Clue come. She really wants to meet Honey, the dog star," I said.

"So, two kids and their dog are getting into the party," Roger said, "and I'm *not*?"

"Sorry, Roger," Mr. Martinez said. "Tonight we are going to find out which actors are up to win Holly awards. You're not an actor. You're a stuntman. And stuntmen weren't invited."

"We'll see about that!" Roger yelled. Then he turned and stormed off.

Mr. Martinez stared after him for a moment. Then he gave Ashley and me a big smile. "You two shouldn't be standing around out here. Go inside. Enjoy yourselves!"

Ashley held up her camera. "I can't wait to get pictures of all the stars!"

"Oh, cameras aren't allowed inside the party," Mr. Martinez told her. He held out his hand, and Ashley gave him the camera.

"I'll give it back to you later," he promised.

"Let's ask Justin to take a picture with us *after* the party," Ashley whispered to me.

"Good idea," I said. "We can't go back home without that picture for Patty."

Ashley, Clue, and I stepped through a doorway and entered the ballroom of the hotel. Clue gave a loud woof.

Ashley patted our brown-and-white basset hound's head. "Clue is excited to be here, too."

"Look! The Holly awards!" I pointed to a table at the front of the room. The Hollys looked like small, old-fashioned microphones dipped in gold. The base of each statue was covered with sparkly rhinestones. An extra-big Holly sat next to the others.

"That big one is for Entertainer of the Year," Ashley said. "I bet Justin will win that award for sure!"

"Mmm-hmm," I mumbled. I was busy

staring at a boy on the dance floor. He was tall with blond hair. *Could it be? Yes!*

"Ashley! Justin Dare is right over there!" I bounced up and down on my toes.

"It's really him this time," Ashley said.

"Let's ask him about the picture," I said.

"We have to wait until he finishes dancing with—" Ashley's eyes got really wide. "I don't believe it! He's dancing with Glory Daniels."

"I love her," I said. "Remember how amazing she was in *Princess in Pink*?"

"Justin and Glory dancing together. I can't wait to tell Patty!" Ashley said.

We watched Justin twirl Glory around and around. They were great dancers.

Ashley gasped. "Did you see that?"

"Yup. That was an amazing spin," I said.

"No, not *that*," she whispered. "Justin just stole Glory's necklace!"

I stared hard at Justin. He was slipping Glory's ruby necklace into the pocket of his tuxedo. "You're right!" I cried. I couldn't believe it!

"This is horrible!" Ashley said. "Justin didn't just play a thief in the movie. He's a thief in real life!"

2

STOP, THIEF!

"What are we going to do?" I said to Ashley.

"What *can* we do?" Ashley said. "We have to tell Mr. Martinez that we saw Justin Dare steal a necklace."

The song ended. Glory gave Justin a kiss on the cheek and started to walk away.

"Oh, Glorrrrrr-yyyyyy," Justin called. His voice was so loud that everyone in the ballroom could hear him. "Did you lose something?"

"I don't think so," Glory answered.

Justin pulled the ruby necklace out of his pocket. "What about *this*?"

Everyone in the ballroom gasped.

Glory touched her neck. "How did you do that?" she asked.

"Oh, it's just a little something I learned while making *Teen Thief*," he said with a grin.

Everyone started to applaud. Justin bowed and gave the necklace back to Glory. I clapped until my hands hurt.

"Now he *definitely* deserves to win the Entertainer of the Year award," Ashley said.

Clue gave a long, loud woof. She agreed too!

"Okay. Let's talk to him now," I said. Ashley and I hurried over to Justin before he started dancing again.

"We love you," Ashley blurted out. Then her face turned bright red.

"You were great in *Teen Thief*," I added.

"Thanks," Justin said. "I worked really hard on that part."

"We could tell," Ashley answered. "We saw you steal Glory's necklace. We thought you were a real thief!"

Justin laughed. "It's all acting," he said. "I did most of my own stunts in the movie. It was so much fun. Do you remember the part—"

Justin didn't have time to finish. A drum-roll interrupted him. A pink spotlight suddenly lit up the front of the Holly awards table.

Mr. Martinez stepped into the light. He was holding a microphone. "It's time to announce the Holly award finalists," he said.

"Excuse me," Justin whispered to us. "I should go up there. I have a feeling that my name is going to be called." He disappeared into the crowd.

"We'll have to ask him about the picture later," Ashley said.

Mr. Martinez announced the finalists for all of the Holly awards. "And now, what you've all been waiting for," he continued. "The performers up for the Entertainer of the Year award are…" Another drumroll sounded. "Clive Wallace, Glory Daniels, Sissy Jordan, William O'Brian, and Billy Bluth."

"Justin is a better actor than everyone else put together," Ashley cried. "And he's not up for one single award!"

I was disappointed too. I saw Justin hang his head and slowly walk away from the Holly table.

Then Clue started wagging her tail. She let out a loud bark and tugged on her leash.

"Clue, what is it, girl?" I got my answer when I saw a honey-colored golden retriever across the room. "Hey, Ashley. I think Clue sees *her* favorite movie star."

"Honey!" Ashley exclaimed. "Let's go say hi."

Clue pulled us toward Honey, who was

sitting at the base of a grand staircase. When we reached the dog star, Clue and Honey touched noses. They both wagged their tails.

The woman who was holding Honey's leash smiled at us. "Honey likes your dog," she said.

"Clue likes Honey, too," Ashley answered. "And we all like Honey's movies!"

A girl who looked as if she was about our age was standing next to the woman. She had long black hair. "That's why Honey should have been one of the finalists for Entertainer of the Year," she said, stamping her foot. "Everyone loves her!"

"I'm Kathy Rice, and this is my daughter, Amanda," the woman said. "Amanda helps me train Honey."

"I'm Ashley, and this is my sister, Mary-Kate," Ashley said.

Amanda planted her hands on her hips. "Don't *you* think Honey is better than any of those five finalists?"

"Amanda, you know dogs can't win Holly awards," Amanda's mother said. "Honey loves being an actress. And you love teaching her tricks. She doesn't need an award."

Mrs. Rice handed Honey's leash to Amanda. "I have to run upstairs for a minute. Please hold on to Honey for me," she said as she headed up the staircase.

Honey put her paws on the first step and whimpered.

"Honey is afraid of heights. She won't climb stairs. She won't even go into an elevator," Amanda explained.

She gave Honey a pat on the head. "Mom doesn't understand. Honey isn't just a dog that does tricks. She is a star. People go to the movies just to see her. Honey deserves a Holly more than anybody here."

"She *is* great," Ashley agreed.

"Watch this," Amanda said. She flicked her hand toward the ground. Honey lay down right away. Then Amanda wiggled her fingers. Honey covered her nose with one paw and began to whimper.

Clue gave her a lick on the nose. "Clue thinks Honey is really sad," I told Amanda.

"That's because Honey is the best actress in the world," Amanda bragged. "She can be angry, sad, scared, anything!"

Amanda waved at a waiter, and he hurried over to us. "Honey deserves a treat," she said. "Caviar is her favorite." Amanda filled a silver spoon with the shiny black fish eggs and held it down for Honey.

"And these are my favorite." Amanda took a star-shaped cookie covered with gold icing. "Don't you two want anything?"

I reached for a cookie. But my hand froze in the air when I saw the waiter's face. "You're not a waiter!" I cried.

3

MOVIE-STAR MADNESS

"You're Roger, Justin Dare's stuntman!" Ashley exclaimed.

Roger Lorre lifted his chin. "I'm an actor," he announced. "I don't only do stunts. I *become* the character."

He leaned down and scratched Honey behind her silky ears. "I was hoping to talk to you tonight," he said to Amanda. "I would love to do a movie with Honey sometime."

Amanda shook her head. "Honey is a star," she told Roger firmly. "That means she works only with other stars—not stuntmen."

Amanda took the last cookie on the tray and fed it to Honey. "Honey needs a walk. I'll be back in a few minutes." She headed toward the front door.

"Come back!" Roger yelled after her. "You don't understand. I *am* a star. I did all the stunts in *Teen Thief*. They should give *me* a Holly!"

Justin Dare stomped over to us. "I asked you to stop telling those lies," he said. "You were hardly in my movie!"

"Give me a break. I was in every single scene!" Roger shouted. "Who walked the tightrope between two buildings? Who rode on the wing of an airplane? Me! That's who!"

"Oh, yeah? Well, you're not even supposed to be at this party," Justin yelled. "Why don't you go home!"

"*You* go home!" Roger gave Justin a big shove.

Justin stumbled and crashed into the table holding the Hollys. The Hollys toppled and fell to the floor.

"Look what you made me do!" Justin launched himself at Roger. The two boys went flying into a waiter carrying a tray full of drinks.

Crash! The crystal glasses shattered on the floor. People screamed and rushed out of the way.

Clue howled. "It's okay, Clue," I said. "Everything's fine."

Amanda hurried over and shoved Honey's leash into my hands. "I have to find my mom. Hold on to Honey, okay?"

Honey tugged on the leash as the two boys continued to fight. She pulled so hard, I thought she was going to pull my hand right off.

"Ashley, help!" We both grabbed Honey and held on tight.

Finally Mr. Martinez and another man

broke up the fight. "I think it's time for you *both* to go home," he said to the boys.

Justin exited to the left. And Roger stomped off to the right.

People milled around the room, chattering about the fight.

A few minutes later, Amanda's mom returned. "Where is Amanda?" she asked.

"She went to find you," Ashley said.

"Oh. Okay," Mrs. Rice said. "Well, thank you for watching Honey," she added, taking Honey's leash.

"No problem," I said.

"Attention, everyone!" Mr. Martinez tapped on the microphone to get the crowd's attention. His face was pinched into a worried look. "Everyone, stay where you are!" he cried.

Ashley and I froze. What was going on?

"Nobody move," he said. "The Entertainer of the Year award has been stolen!"

4

A DUMB CLUE

Ashley, Clue, and I ran to Mr. Martinez's side. "We can help," I told him.

"I hope so," Mr. Martinez said. "The Holly awards show is in two days. I have to get the Entertainer of the Year statue back before then!"

"Don't worry," Ashley said. "The Olsen and Olsen detective team is on the case!"

"Let's get to work," I told Ashley. I led the way to the table where the Holly awards had been standing. The floor was littered with food and bits of broken glass.

"The crime scene is a mess," I said. "It's going to be tough to find clues."

"We just have to take things slowly," Ashley said.

Yup. That was my sister, all right. The two of us may look a lot alike, but we are different in many ways. Ashley likes to think and think and think and *think* about every clue. I like to jump right in and *do* things.

"Okay, Clue," I said. "Time to use your super-duper snooper."

"Woof!" Clue sniffed the floor of the crime scene.

I stepped carefully around the glass and ice on the floor.

Whoever stole the Holly had to make a quick getaway, I thought to myself.

"What's this for?" Ashley asked. She was standing by a small door in the middle of a nearby wall. She swung open the door and leaned inside. "It looks like a big cabinet set right into the wall."

"What's in there?" I asked. I scooped up Clue and joined Ashley.

"Just a few crumbs of food," Ashley replied. "Wait. There's something else."

I pulled a plastic evidence bag from my pocket and handed it to Ashley. Our great-grandma Olive taught us that a good detective is always prepared. She's a detective, too.

Ashley turned and opened her hand. In her palm sat three tiny sparkly stones. She dropped the stones inside the bag. "I'll be right back," she said. "I've got to check something out."

"I'll search this cabinet some more," I said.

I leaned inside and ran my hands along the walls. The cabinet was big enough for a person to fit inside.

Or for a thief to hide *in*, I thought.

Next I ran my fingers around the edges of the door. Something tickled my left pinkie. Hairs! Blond hairs were stuck on the door.

Another clue! I pulled out another evidence bag and slid the hairs into it.

"Excuse me." A waitress stepped in front of me and put a tray of dirty dishes in the cabinet. Then she closed the door and pushed a button on the wall. The cabinet began to hum.

"What is that?" I asked. "Some kind of dishwasher?"

"It's called a dumbwaiter," the waitress said. "It's like a little elevator. The kitchen sends trays of food up here in the dumbwaiter. And we use it to send the dirty dishes back down."

"Cool," I said.

"It beats carrying trays up and down the stairs!" the waitress agreed. She headed off.

A second later Ashley rushed back up to

me. "I just found out something!" I told her.

"So did I." Ashley held out the Holly for Best Movie. Then she shook the stones in the evidence bag. "See these? They're rhinestones—and they look just like the ones on the other Hollys."

I gasped. "That means the thief put the Entertainer of the Year award in here!" I said. "It's called a dumbwaiter. It's a mini-elevator. Maybe the thief even used it to escape."

"That means the thief could be down in the kitchen right now!" Ashley said.

"Come on!" I cried, heading for the stairs to the kitchen. "Maybe we can still catch the crook!"

5

CLUE FINDS A CLUE

Ashley and I raced down the steps. We burst through the kitchen's big swinging doors...

...and an iron frying pan came flying right at us!

"Duck!" Ashley yelled.

The frying pan hit the wall right above our heads. It clattered to the floor.

"I won't stand for this!" A man in a tall white hat grabbed a saucepan. He threw it at the big refrigerator. "I am the chef here!

And I tell you my kitchen is the cleanest in the entire city!"

"I'm sorry, sir," a woman in a gray suit told the chef. "But it is my job to make sure that restaurant kitchens are in order. And what I've found in here is unacceptable."

"Excuse me," I said. "But did anyone see a person jump out of the dumbwaiter with a Holly award?"

The chef gasped. So did the woman.

"Get that filthy dog out of my kitchen!" the chef cried.

I glanced at Clue. "She's not dirty. Ashley and I gave her a bath this morning!"

"Out!" the chef yelled. "Out! Out! Out!"

"Mary-Kate, look!" Ashley pointed to a door across the room. A red sign above it read EMERGENCY EXIT. The door was halfway open. "The thief probably took the Holly right out that door!"

Ashley, Clue, and I bolted through the emergency exit—and into an alley.

There was no sign of the thief.

"We're too late," I said.

"The thief could be anywhere by now." Ashley sighed. "I wish we had another clue."

Clue turned to Ashley and began to whimper.

"Don't worry, Clue. She didn't mean another *dog*," I said, patting her on the head. Then I remembered something. "Wait! There *is* another clue!"

"Really?" Ashley said. "Tell me! Tell me!"

"Well, I know for a fact that the thief has blond hair," I said proudly.

"How do you know that?" Ashley asked.

I pulled out the evidence bag with the blond hairs in it. "I found these in the dumb-waiter. That means our thief is blond."

Ashley shook her head. "But how do we know that these hairs came from the thief? They could be from a waitress or somebody else."

"Oh," I said. I hadn't thought of that.

"But, then again," Ashley said slowly, "the thief must have been in a hurry to leave the ballroom. So there is a good chance that a thief *would* catch his hair in the dumbwaiter. We should check it out."

"Cool!" I said. "It's time to make a list of suspects."

"Right." Ashley grabbed a small notebook and pencil out of her pocket. She carried them everywhere—just in case we needed to solve a mystery.

"Roger Lorre was upset because he didn't get invited to the party. Maybe he stole the Holly to ruin it for everyone else," I said. "*And* he has blond hair."

Ashley wrote down his name. "Justin Dare has blond hair, too," she said. "Maybe he took the Entertainer of the Year award because he wasn't a finalist. He seemed really disappointed."

I didn't want Justin to be the thief. I knew Ashley didn't either. But I had to say what I was thinking. "And Justin is good at stealing," I said. "We saw him take Glory's necklace."

"You're right." Ashley nodded and put a star next to Justin's name. "But maybe Roger is good at stealing, too. Remember? He told us about the stunt where he climbed up the Empire State Building with *stolen* coins."

"Roger could have taken the award right after his argument with Justin," I said. "And then used the dumbwaiter to make his escape through the kitchen. Everybody was busy talking about the fight. Nobody was paying attention."

Ashley sighed. "Yeah. But that means Justin could have done the same thing. They're both really good suspects."

"Grrrrrrr," Clue growled. She was sniffing the ground near the door.

"Mary-Kate, look!" Ashley said. "I think Clue found another clue!"

THE CARDBOARD ACTOR

Ashley and I ran over to Clue. "What is it, Clue? What did you find?" I asked.

Right under Clue's nose was a white piece of paper. I snatched it up.

Ashley leaned over my shoulder. "It's a business card for a photographer," she said.

"Way to go, Clue!" I cried. "I'll bet the thief dropped this!"

"It's possible, but anyone could have dropped it," Ashley said. "Let's check it out tomorrow, okay? If Roger has been to this photographer, that makes him a better suspect."

"Justin could have dropped it, too," I added sadly. "Let's head back to the party and say good-bye to Mr. Martinez. We'll get a fresh start in the morning."

"Good idea," Ashley said.

When we entered the ballroom, it was almost empty.

Mr. Martinez came over to us. "No one seems to be in a party mood anymore," he said. "How is the case coming along?"

"We found some good clues," Ashley said. "We're going to check them out first thing in the morning."

"Thanks, girls," he said. "If anyone can solve this mystery, you can."

We said good-bye to Mr. Martinez and crossed the ballroom to the door. Amanda was there, tying little suede booties onto Honey's paws.

"I guess Amanda's mom found her," I said. "Amanda's got Honey now."

"Yeah." Ashley looked thoughtful. "You know, Amanda has a great motive, too," she said. "She's mad because her dog can't win a Holly."

"But Amanda has black hair, not blond," I reminded her.

Ashley pulled out her detective notebook. She quickly wrote Amanda's name on the list of suspects anyway.

"She's a suspect. Just not a great suspect," Ashley said. "It can't hurt to question her."

But when we reached Amanda and Honey, Clue began to growl.

"Down, girl," I said. I gripped Clue's leash a little tighter.

Clue didn't listen. Instead, she barked and barked and barked.

"What's wrong?" I tried to hold Clue back. "You love Honey, remember?"

Honey growled and tugged at her leash.

"Hey!" Amanda cried.

Woof! Woof! Woof! Woof! Woof!

"Clue, what is it?" I cried, pulling her away.

"Heel!" Amanda told Honey.

Both dogs finally stopped barking. Clue sat next to my feet. Honey sat down beside Amanda.

"Don't worry," Amanda said to Honey. "As soon as Mom comes back with the car, we're out of here."

She turned to us. "I think your dog is jealous," she said. "Clue probably wishes she got to wear special dog shoes and eat caviar." She fed Honey a bone-shaped treat from her pocket.

Clue let out a growl. Then she started barking again.

"Our dog is not like that," Ashley said— even though it *did* seem as if it were true.

"Maybe we should go," I said, and led Clue to the door.

Ashley followed. "Let's get Clue some

doggie treats at the store tomorrow," she whispered.

"Don't worry," I told Clue. "You don't have to be jealous of Honey. You're special, too. You're a *detective*."

"Cool! Look at the stars on the sidewalk!" Ashley exclaimed the next morning.

We were hurrying down Hollywood Boulevard, staring at the big gold stars that were set into the sidewalk. Each star had a famous person's name printed on it.

"Hey! Here's Johnny Sparkle's star," I said.

"Do you think Justin Dare will ever have a star?" Ashley asked.

"He should!" I answered. "Unless—"

"Unless he's the thief," Ashley finished for me.

I nodded. "Then it wouldn't be fair for him to have a star."

My stomach started to hurt. I really, *really* didn't want Justin to be the guilty one. But a good detective has to investigate all the suspects.

"Look! There's the photographer's studio," Ashley announced.

"I sure hope Justin hasn't been here," I said.

Ashley opened the door to the studio. Then she stopped so fast that I ran into her. "Justin has definitely been here," she told me.

"How do you know?" I asked.

Clue and I followed Ashley inside. A life-size cardboard cutout of Justin stood against one wall. Yes. Justin had definitely been here. And that made him an even better suspect.

A man with red hair tied back in a pony-tail came up to us. "Hello, girls," he said. "Are you Justin Dare fans? I could take your picture with him," he offered.

"I wonder if Patty would believe—" Ashley began.

"She would know it wasn't the real

Justin," I said to Ashley. "But thanks anyway," I told the photographer.

"So, have you really met Justin Dare?" Ashley asked him.

"He's in here all the time," the photographer answered. "In fact, he stopped in this morning on his way to the movie studio."

"What about Honey's trainer, Amanda?" I burst out. "Has she ever brought Honey here?"

Please say yes, I thought. I didn't want the evidence to point only to Justin.

The photographer shook his head. His ponytail swung back and forth. "No," he said. "But I'd like to take pictures of Honey. She has such beautiful fur."

"Our dog has beautiful fur, too," Ashley said, petting Clue.

"Yes, she does," the photographer agreed. "And I love her long ears. I could take a picture of all three of you with the cardboard Justin."

"No thanks," Ashley answered.

The photographer shrugged. "You seemed like big fans."

"We are," Ashley and I said together.

"Then maybe you'd like to know who was in here just yesterday," the photographer said.

"Who?" Ashley asked.

"Justin Dare's stuntman," he replied.

"Roger Lorre was here?" I said.

"You really *are* fans," the photographer said. "Most people don't even know Justin has a stunt double."

"Why was Roger here?" Ashley asked.

"Actors need pictures of themselves to take on auditions. Roger wants to be an actor, just like Justin," the photographer explained. He smiled at us. "Now, what can I do for you two?"

"Oh, you've helped us enough already," I said. "Thanks a lot."

"Anytime." The photographer shrugged

again as we headed out the door. "Good-bye!"

As soon as we hit the sidewalk, Ashley started writing in her detective notebook.

"Justin and Roger are still our two best suspects," I said.

"You're right," Ashley agreed. "And you know what that means."

"What?" I asked.

Ashley grinned. "Our next stop is a real live movie studio!"

7

SNEAKING AROUND

"This is it! Sunburst Studios," I announced. I stared up at the huge gates in front of the studio. Each half had a big metal sun on it.

"It looks like we go in through there." Ashley pointed to a small building to the left of the gates. A group of people stood outside the gates, waiting to go in. Ashley and I got in line behind a teenage girl with long brown braids.

"I can't believe we're going to see Justin

Dare!" the girl squealed, jumping up and down.

"I know," her friend answered. "All we have to do is find Trailer Twenty-five. My dad's hairstylist's baby-sitter is a friend of Justin's cousin. She swore that it's Justin's trailer."

Ashley wrote "Trailer 25" in her detective notebook. The line moved forward. Ashley and I stepped inside the building. I spotted a long counter with a security guard standing behind it.

A man with a little girl moved up to the counter.

"What is your business at the studio today?" the guard asked.

"*Carrots and Sunglasses* audition," the man answered.

"Sign here," the security guard told him.

The man signed a piece of paper on a clipboard.

The guard handed him a pair of sunglasses and bunny ears from behind the counter. "Good luck," he said, and waved for them to move on.

The girls in front of us stepped up to the counter. "What is your business at the studio today?" the guard asked.

"We're here to see Mr. Dare." The girl flipped her braids behind her shoulders. "It's very important."

The guard picked up a clipboard. "Name?" he asked.

"I'm a very good friend of Mr. Dare's," she answered. "I mean, of *Justin's*."

"I need a name." The guard held up a clipboard. "And you have to be on this list. Or you don't get in."

The girls gave him their names, but they weren't on the list.

"Sorry," the guard said. "You'll have to leave."

"What are we going to do?" I asked Ashley. "Our names aren't on that list either."

"We're going in as bunnies," she said. "Just follow me."

"What is your business at the studio?" the guard asked when we reached the counter.

"Uh, *Carrots and*—uh…uh…" Ashley stammered.

"*Carrots and Sunflowers!*" I burst out. I was pretty sure that's what the man with the little girl had said.

"*Carrots and Sunglasses?*" the guard asked.

"Yes!" I said. "Yes! We're here for that."

The guard raised one eyebrow. "Aren't you two a little old to be on that show?"

"We're…tall for our age," Ashley explained.

The guard stared at us for a moment.

I crossed my fingers. I crossed my toes. *Please let us in*, I thought. *Please, please, please!*

"Sign here," he said.

My fingers shook as I signed my name. Ashley signed, too. Then the guard handed us two pairs of sunglasses and bunny ears.

"Uh, we need one more," I told him.

"Huh? For who?" he asked.

I pointed at Clue. "Don't worry, I'll sign for her."

The guard rolled his eyes and handed me sunglasses and bunny ears for Clue. Then he waved us through the gates.

Ashley slapped me a high five when we were out of sight. "Now all we have to do is find Trailer Twenty-five!"

We put on our bunny ears and sunglasses and looked around the movie studio. It was awesome!

There was a big fake sunset painted on the side of one whole building. In front of it was a huge tank of water. It was big enough to fit ten swimming pools!

"They must film underwater scenes in there," I said.

"Excuse me," Ashley called to a person in a werewolf costume who was passing by. "Do you know where Trailer Twenty-five is?"

The werewolf pointed straight ahead. "Go through New York City and turn right at the Empire State Building." The werewolf rushed away before we could ask any more questions.

"New York City?" I repeated. "But we're in California."

"Look! There's a building that looks like the Empire State Building over there," Ashley replied.

"It must be a set. They're probably filming a movie that takes place in New York City," I said.

"Let's go," Ashley said. We headed toward the building. "This is so strange. There are all these stores and everything. But no one is inside."

"Maybe they aren't making a movie in

New York City today," I answered. We reached the Empire State Building. "Wow! It's not as tall as the real one, but it looks just like it. Cool!"

We turned right at the building. A big parking lot stretched out in front of us. The lot was filled with long trailers.

I peeked in the window of the closest one. Inside I saw a sofa, a little fridge, a coffee table, a TV set, and a bed.

"I think the actors go into these trailers when they need a break," Ashley said. She ran her fingers over the numbers on the door. "This is nineteen. We should be close to Justin's trailer."

She was right. Trailer number twenty-five was in the next row. Ashley, Clue, and I crept closer. We could hear someone talking inside.

"I'd like to thank my parents, of course. And my little sister. And my fabulous director."

I knew that voice. It was Justin Dare!

"Who is he talking to?" Ashley whispered.

"Let's find out." I tiptoed up to the window and looked inside.

"Most of all, I'd like to thank my fans," Justin said. He flashed a smile into a mirror hanging on the wall. "I wouldn't have won the Entertainer of the Year award without them."

"Oh, no!" I whispered.

Justin Dare was talking to himself. And he was holding the stolen Holly!

CAUGHT!

Justin was the thief! And the stolen Holly award was in his trailer right this second!

Ashley grabbed my arm. "Someone is coming!"

We turned around and pretended to be waiting for someone at the trailer across from Justin's. We watched as a guy in a baseball cap knocked on Justin's door. "We need you on the set, Mr. Dare," the guy called.

The trailer door swung open and Justin

stepped out. Ashley and I waited until Justin was out of sight. Then we ran back to the trailer. Justin had left the door wide open.

"What luck!" I said, and led the way inside.

The Holly that Justin had been holding sat on the coffee table. Ashley picked it up carefully. "You're not going to believe this!"

She held up the award. "This isn't a real Holly!" she said. She turned the statue so I could see the front of it. "Read what it says."

"'World's Best Brother,'" I read aloud. "It's like the trophies you find in a gift shop. Justin is innocent!"

"We don't know that for sure," Ashley said. "Let's check out the rest of the trailer."

"It feels wrong to be snooping around Justin Dare's stuff," I said. I looked inside the fridge. There were two bottles of water and an apple inside. But no Holly in sight.

"I know," Ashley agreed. "But we have to do our job." She flipped through the pile of magazines on the coffee table. Then she peered under the sofa. "Nothing," she announced.

I checked under the bed. Then under the pillows on the bed. "Nothing," I said.

Ashley looked behind the TV. "Nothing."

We searched the tiny bathroom together. We didn't find a single clue.

"Should we wait and talk to Justin when he comes back?" I asked.

"No, we don't have time." Ashley checked her watch. "We have only thirty-three hours left before the Holly awards show. And we need to visit Roger Lorre's house."

"Okay." I grabbed Clue's leash and we all headed out of the trailer.

"Hey!" someone shouted as we stepped out the door. "Mary-Kate and Ashley Olsen! What are you doing?"

9

A Hairy Good Clue

"**O**h, no," Ashley said. "We're caught!"

We looked across the lot and saw Amanda and Honey.

Clue wagged her tail as they walked up to us.

"What are you two doing here wearing those ridiculous bunny ears?" Amanda asked.

I yanked off my rabbit ears and my sunglasses. I'd forgotten all about them! Then I reached over and took off Clue's ears while Ashley took off hers.

"We were just, um…" I began.

"Pretending to be bunnies," Ashley added. "I guess we've got the acting bug."

Amanda shrugged. "Well, Honey and I were about to get lunch," she said. "Honey has her own chef here at the studio. Do you want to come?"

"Thanks, but we have to go," Ashley told her.

"It's probably just as well," Amanda answered. "We don't want Clue to get jealous again."

I looked down at Clue. She and Honey were giving each other nose kisses. "I don't think you have to worry about that," I said. But it was kind of weird. How come Clue and Honey were friends again?

"Come on, Honey. You're having steak today!" Amanda gave us a wave and headed toward the Empire State Building.

We waved good-bye, too, and left the studio.

We found a phone booth outside the Sunburst gates. Roger Lorre was listed in the phone book.

A half hour and two buses later, the three of us were standing on Roger Lorre's front porch. I knocked on the door.

Roger jerked the door open. He was wearing plastic gloves, and he had a shower cap on his head. There was a funny smell in the air. Clue sneezed.

"Hello there!" Roger said. "Do you girls want my autograph after all?"

Ashley and I stared. We knew it was rude, but Roger looked so funny—we couldn't help it. Under the cap, we could see that half his hair was blond and half was brown.

"What's that on your head?" I asked.

Roger reached up and adjusted his shower cap. "Oh, this? I'm in the middle of touching up my hair. What can I do for you girls?"

"We'd like to ask you a few questions about last night," Ashley said.

"Okay. Come in." Roger went over to a big mirror in the hallway and picked up a spray can. He shook it hard.

"Did you know that the Entertainer of the Year award was stolen right after you left?" I asked.

"No way!" Roger gasped. "It was *stolen*?" He took off his shower cap. Then he pointed the can at his hair and sprayed.

The brown parts of his hair slowly turned blond.

"You spray-paint your hair?" I asked.

"This isn't paint," Roger told me. "It's an all natural vegetable dye. It washes right out with water. And the color is exactly like—" He clamped his mouth shut.

"Like Justin Dare's?" Ashley asked.

"I happen to like blond hair," Roger said. He kept on spraying. "Do you know who took the Holly award?" he asked.

"Not yet," Ashley answered. "Do you think we could use your bathroom for a minute?"

"Sure. It's down the hall to the right," Roger told us.

Ashley and I hurried down the hall and into the bathroom. "You have the hair samples from the dumbwaiter, right?" Ashley asked.

I pulled the evidence out of my pocket. Ashley took it from me and turned on the cold water in the sink.

"What are you doing, Ashley?"

"We have to see if the blond on these hairs washes out," she said. "Because if it does, Roger Lorre is our thief!"

MINUS ONE SUSPECT

I leaned over the sink and locked my eyes on the hairs. I really wanted them to turn brown. If they did, that meant that Roger was the thief and Justin was innocent!

Ashley ran the water over the hairs. She rubbed the hairs between her fingers. Nothing happened.

"They still look blond," I said. "Do it again."

Ashley let the water run over the hairs for a full minute. But the hairs stayed blond.

Ashley put the evidence back into the bag and handed it to me. Then she crossed Roger's name off the suspect list in her notebook.

"You know what this means, don't you?" she said.

I did. It meant that Justin Dare was our number one suspect.

"Usually this would be so much fun," I said to Ashley the next morning. "Here we are. In Hollywood. Taking a tour of the stars' homes in a cool double-decker bus."

"I know," Ashley agreed. "But maybe when we get to Justin's house we won't find any evidence against him. We aren't totally sure he's guilty."

"But he has blond hair," I reminded her. "And he gets his pictures taken at the photography studio that was on the business card we found. *And* he knows how to steal. *And* he's upset that he can't win the

Entertainer of the Year statue at the Holly awards show tonight."

"I know, I know." Ashley frowned. She checked the map. "Justin's house is next."

The bus pulled to a stop. The door opened with a whoosh of air. Ashley, Clue, and I climbed out with the rest of the tourists.

"Remember, no walking on the grass," the bus driver called. "You can take pictures from the sidewalk. That's it."

Ashley, Clue, and I ducked behind a tree. We hid there until everyone returned to the bus. We waited until the bus drove away.

"Time to talk to Justin," Ashley said. She smoothed her hair down. I fixed my hair, too. Then we walked straight up to Justin's front door and rang the bell.

A tall man opened the door. "Can I help you?" he asked.

"We need to see Justin," I told him.

"Mr. Dare isn't here," the man answered. "I'm the head of his security team. Let me tell you right now that no one sees Mr. Dare without an appointment. If you don't have an appointment, please don't come back."

The man shut the door before Ashley or I could say anything. "The awards ceremony is in less than eight hours. What are we going to do?" I groaned.

"I guess we should head back to our hotel," she said. "We need some thinking time."

"And we need some ice cream. That always helps me think," I said.

Two buses later, we were back at our hotel. "It's hard to believe this is where the party was last night," Ashley said as we headed inside.

"No crowd of people. No excitement in the air," I said. Ashley and I walked through the lobby and headed straight for the restaurant.

I groaned when I saw the sign on the front door. "Closed! I can't believe it."

"There's a notice from that health inspector we saw in the kitchen the other night," Ashley said. She pointed to the window. "It says the restaurant is closed until next week—until the kitchen is cleaned properly."

"I guess we'll have to do our thinking without ice cream," I said. We headed for the elevator and went up to our room.

"Hey, someone left us a present!" I said. I pointed to a big basket sitting on Ashley's bed.

Ashley ran over and grabbed the basket. "It's from Great-grandma Olive! She sent tapes of all the movies that are up for Holly awards. Do you want to watch *Teen Thief* again?" she asked.

"I don't want to look at Justin Dare right now," I answered. "What else is there?"

"Honey's latest movie, *Doggie to the Rescue*," Ashley answered. "Glory Daniels is in it, too."

"Cool! Let's watch that," I told her. Ashley handed me the tape. I stuck it into the VCR and pushed PLAY.

Ashley flopped onto her bed. Clue and I stretched out on mine. All three of us watched the movie.

"Go, Honey!" Ashley called to the TV.

It was a pretty exciting part of the movie. Honey was inching along the edge of a cliff. Then she spotted a doll lying on a rock a few feet below.

Clue gave a bark.

"Be careful, Honey!" I said as the dog started toward the doll.

Slowly, Honey crept out onto the rock. She was so high up, it was really scary. I covered my eyes, but I also wanted to see what was going to happen. So I peeked through my fingers.

Honey picked up the doll with her mouth. Then she slid it into the side pocket of a pouch strapped to her back.

"She made it!" Ashley exclaimed.

On the screen, Honey ran back to the top of the cliff.

I sat straight up. "Wait a second!" I grabbed the remote and pressed PAUSE.

"What's wrong?" Ashley asked.

"Nothing," I said with a grin. "But I think I just figured out who stole the Holly!"

11

A New Suspect?

"Who?" Ashley jumped off her bed. "Who stole the Holly?"

"Amanda said Honey is afraid of heights, right?" I asked.

Ashley nodded. "Go on."

"Well, if Honey is so scared, then how can she do *this*?"

I pressed PLAY on the remote control. The TV showed Honey trotting up the cliff to give the doll back to a little girl.

"Amanda totally lied about that!" I said.

"And what color hair does Honey have?"

"Blond!" Ashley shouted.

"Right!" I said. "It all adds up. Amanda and Honey stole the award." I closed my eyes, trying to picture how they did it.

"Amanda probably placed the award in Honey's mouth. I bet that's how those rhinestones came loose. She helped Honey into the dumbwaiter, then sent it downstairs so Honey could make a quick escape. Then Amanda ran downstairs to the kitchen. She let Honey out of the dumbwaiter. Then they both escaped through the alley."

"Good work, Mary-Kate." Ashley was just about to give me a high five when she groaned. "Oh, no!"

"What's the matter?" I asked. "The case is closed."

Ashley shook her head. "But we were holding Honey when the Holly was stolen," she said. "Amanda and Honey couldn't have taken the award. There's just no way."

"Looks like the case is open again." I sighed. "And Justin is our number one suspect again."

I leaned back on my pillow. On the TV, I watched Honey leap into the back of a pickup truck. The little girl sat next to her, clutching her doll.

Why would Amanda lie to us about Honey for no reason? Why would she tell us Honey was afraid of heights? I wondered.

I couldn't come up with an answer. And another thing bothered me, too. Why did Clue sometimes like Honey and sometimes not? It just didn't make sense.

The phone rang. I reached over and grabbed it. "Hello?"

"So, do you have the picture?" a familiar voice demanded.

"It's Patty," I told Ashley.

"Do you have the picture with you and Ashley and Justin Dare?" Patty asked.

We didn't have the picture. And there was no way we were going to get it. How could we? Justin Dare was probably going to be in trouble as soon as Ashley and I solved this case.

"Well?" Patty said.

"We've got a picture with Roger Lorre," I burst out. Roger had insisted that we take a photo with him before we left his house.

"Who is Roger Lorre?" Patty asked.

"He's Justin Dare's stunt double. He did a lot of stunts in *Teen Thief.* And he looks a lot like Justin," I rushed on. "Ashley and I even thought he was Justin at first."

"Mary-Kate, a picture with Justin Dare's *stunt double* does *not* count," Patty said.

Stunt double. The words repeated in my head. *Stunt double...stunt double...*

I leaped to my feet. Ashley blinked at me in surprise. "Patty, I have to go! Right now! 'Bye!"

I hung up before Patty could say another

word. "Ashley, put on Clue's leash. We have to get her over to Amanda's right away!"

"Why?" Ashley asked.

"Amanda and Honey may not have stolen the Holly," I said. "But I have a hunch I know who did!"

12

DOUBLE THE HONEY

"**Y**ou know the plan, right, Ashley?" I asked. We were standing outside Amanda's house.

"You bet," Ashley said. She rang the doorbell.

I reached out and rang it, too. I couldn't wait to find out if I was right.

The door swung open. Amanda's mother stood there.

She smiled at us. "I remember you girls," she said. "We met at the Holly party."

"That's right," I answered. "We talked to Amanda about training dogs for movies. And my sister and I want to know if our dog has what it takes to be a star."

Clue gave a woof. She definitely looked like a star to me.

"I thought maybe Amanda could try to teach some tricks to Clue. Then Amanda could tell us if she thinks Clue could be in the movies," I went on.

"Come in. I'll get Amanda." Mrs. Rice opened the door wider. Ashley and I stepped inside.

"Keep your eyes on Clue," I whispered to Ashley. "And be ready for anything!"

"Hi," Amanda called. She walked up to us. Honey trotted behind her.

I looked back and forth, from Honey to Clue, from Clue to Honey. Was Clue going to wag her tail or bark this time?

Clue's tail started wagging. She trotted up to Honey and licked her on the ear.

"My mom said you want to know if your dog has what it takes to be a star," Amanda said.

"That's right!" I said. "Could you teach her a trick? Ashley and I think she would be amazing in the movies. But we want to know what you think."

Amanda flipped her long black hair over her shoulders. "Most dogs *don't* have what it takes," she warned us.

"Clue is very smart," Ashley told her.

"And look how cute she is!" I added.

Amanda shrugged. "I'll try to teach her to play dead," she said. "All movie dogs need to do that."

Amanda snapped her fingers. "Clue! Look at me!" she ordered.

Clue didn't look at Amanda. She was staring into the hallway.

I kept my eyes on Clue. So did Ashley.

Clue continued to stare into the hallway. Then she started to growl.

"Go get her, Clue!" I shouted. "Go get the thief!"

Clue barked, then bolted down the hall.

"Come on, Ashley!" I called. We tore after Clue.

Clue sped into a room with a huge indoor pool. Then she ran through a little flap in the back door. We could hear her in the backyard, still barking.

We followed Clue outside.

"What are you doing?" Amanda called from behind me.

Ashley skidded to a stop. I slammed into her. Amanda slammed into me. And Honey slammed into her.

Clue stood in the backyard, facing another golden retriever.

"There's another Honey!" Ashley cried.

13

PICTURE PERFECT
SURPRISE!

It was true. The other dog looked just like Honey.

Clue barked and barked. The other golden retriever spun around and ran across the lawn. It disappeared inside a huge doghouse. Make that a dog *mansion*. Clue ran right after the dog.

"Let's go!" I shouted. Ashley and I entered the doghouse. We crawled through a room filled with squeaky toys. We crawled through a room full of chewie bones. We crawled through a room that had a TV and a VCR!

Ashley turned to me. "This place is bigger than our attic!"

I heard Clue barking and followed the sound. It led me to a room with two huge fluffy dog beds. The Entertainer of the Year award stood on a night table between the beds.

"The Holly!" Ashley cried. She grabbed the statue.

"Good girl, Clue!" I exclaimed. I wished I had a whole pot of caviar to give her.

Clue stopped barking at the other dog and licked my face.

"What's going on in there?" I heard Mrs. Rice call.

"We're coming out," Ashley answered. She led the way out of the dog mansion.

Amanda's face turned bright red when she saw the Holly.

"Where did that come from?" Mrs. Rice

asked Ashley and me. She looked surprised.

Ashley and I both looked at Amanda.

Amanda didn't answer.

"What's that dog's name?" I pointed to the other golden retriever.

"That's Henry," Mrs. Rice answered.

"It's a boy?" I wasn't expecting that.

"Yes. Would you please explain what's going on?" Mrs. Rice asked.

"Henry and Amanda stole the Holly," Ashley announced. "Mary-Kate figured it out all by herself."

I grinned. "No way, Ashley. We did it together." Then I turned to Amanda. "Henry is Honey's stunt double, right?"

Amanda nodded. Even the tips of her ears were red now.

"I had a hunch," I said. "I thought if people actors had stunt doubles, then dogs could too."

"It was Henry who was in the scene on the cliff in *Doggie to the Rescue*," Ashley said. "Honey would have been too scared to climb down and get the doll."

"It's true," Amanda answered. "Honey does all the emotional stuff. She acts sad and happy and mad and everything."

Amanda reached over and hugged Honey. Then she hugged Henry. "Henry does the stunts," she explained. "He can jump over anything. Climb up anything. He's amazing."

"I'm still waiting to hear about the stolen Holly award," Mrs. Rice said.

"Amanda gave it to Henry to steal," I said. "She put Henry in the dumbwaiter and met him in the kitchen. The chef was so busy arguing with the health inspector, he didn't see a thing."

"Is this all true, Amanda?" Mrs. Rice asked. "You stole the Holly award?"

"Yes," Amanda admitted. "I thought Honey and Henry deserved it!" She stared at Ashley, then at me. "I can't believe you guys figured it out."

"Clue did!" I answered. "She knew it before we did."

"Right!" Ashley said. "Clue wagged her tail when she saw Honey. But she barked when she saw Henry!"

"Amanda, what do you have to say for yourself?" Mrs. Rice frowned.

"I didn't plan it or anything," Amanda said. "But I was so angry that my dogs couldn't win a Holly. It wasn't fair! And then Justin and Roger started fighting, and nobody was paying attention. So I decided to take the biggest award—so Honey and Henry could share it."

"But if you didn't plan it, why did you have Henry with you?" I asked.

"I wanted Henry and Honey to both enjoy the party. I was going to switch Honey for Henry after I took Honey for her walk," Amanda explained. "I hid Henry under the Holly awards table."

"Well, I've heard enough," Mrs. Rice said

firmly. "Amanda, go get my car keys. We're returning the Holly right now. And you're going to apologize to everyone."

"I'm very, very sorry," Amanda told Mr. Martinez again that night. We were all standing backstage at the Holly awards ceremony.

Mr. Martinez patted her on the shoulder. "Thank you for telling the truth and for returning the Entertainer of the Year award." Then he turned to Ashley and me. "And thank *you* for solving the mystery," he told us.

"You're welcome," I said, smiling.

Ashley tugged on my arm. "Mary-Kate, Justin Dare is coming this way," she said. "Doesn't he look cute in his tuxedo?"

"He sure does," I agreed. "Did you bring the camera? Maybe we can finally ask him to take a picture with us."

Ashley reached into her bag. "Oh, no! I forgot the camera!" she said.

Justin walked right up to us. "Hey, are you two the detectives who found the missing Holly award?" he asked.

"Yup," I said. "That's us!"

"You guys are *soooo* cool!" he said. His face turned bright red. "I mean, it must be exciting to be famous detectives." He held up a camera. "Would you mind taking a picture with me?"

Ashley and I looked at each other and laughed. Would we *mind* taking a picture with Justin Dare?

"Only if we can have a copy," I said.

"No problem," Justin said. "And if you autograph mine, I'll autograph yours!"

An autographed picture of us with Justin!

As Mr. Martinez held up Justin's camera, I imagined showing the photo to our friend Patty O'Leary.

"Smile!" Mr. Martinez said.

Ashley and I smiled our biggest Hollywood smiles!

Hi from both of us,

Yum! What could be more fun than learning how to make ice cream?

Ashley and I decided to enter the ice cream-making contest at the new ice cream store in town. Whoever won the contest would get a free sundae every week for a year! We were having the best time mixing up all kinds of delicious ingredients.

But then someone stole our ice cream! Turn the page for a sneak peek at *The New Adventures of Mary-Kate & Ashley: The Case of the Sundae Surprise.*

See you next time!

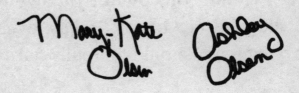

A sneak peek at our next mystery...

The Case Of The
Sundae Surprise

I kept turning the crank on the ice cream maker. It got tougher to turn as the ice cream got colder and harder. "I think it's almost ready," I told my sister Ashley.

"Then it's time for our secret special ingredient, Mary-Kate," Ashley said.

Ashley took a plastic bag out of her backpack. The front of the bag read "The World's Best Gummy Oranges." She measured out a cup of the candy and poured it into our ice cream.

Helen, the owner of Sweet Sundaes, clapped her hands. "Okay, everyone. Your ice cream should be really hard to crank at this point. And that means it's done!"

"Woo-hoo!" Tim cried. "Now comes my favorite part. The eating!"

"Almost," Helen said. "First you need to put your ice cream in one of the buckets." She pointed to a row of buckets on the shelf under the window. "Then I'll need someone to put labels up on the shelf in the freezer. Any volunteers?"

"Mary-Kate and I will do it," Ashley said.

"Great." Helen handed Ashley stick-on labels and a pen. We headed into the big walk-in freezer.

"We should have made the labels in the kitchen. It's freezing in here," Ashley said. She wrote Tim's name on a label and gave it to me.

"That's why they call it a freezer," I teased. I stuck Tim's label on one of the shelves. "Write faster or we'll turn into ice sculptures before we're through."

Ashley filled out the labels at triple

speed. I stuck them on the shelf just as fast. "Done!" I cried.

"Let's get back where it's warm," Ashley said. She shoved on the freezer's big metal door.

It didn't open.

"Let me try." I leaned on the door and pushed as hard as I could.

It didn't open.

Then Ashley and I pushed on the door together. The door still didn't budge.

"We're trapped!" I cried.

THE NEW ADVENTURES OF MARY-KATE & ASHLEY™
Movie Madness Party Sweepstakes

OFFICIAL RULES:

1. No purchase necessary.

2. To enter complete the official entry form or hand print your name, address, age, and phone number along with the words "THE NEW ADVENTURES OF MARY-KATE & ASHLEY Movie Madness Party Sweepstakes" on a 3" x 5" card and mail to: THE NEW ADVENTURES OF MARY-KATE & ASHLEY Movie Madness Party Sweepstakes, c/o HarperEntertainment, Attn: Children's Marketing Department, 10 East 53rd Street, New York, NY 10022. Entries must be received **no later than April 30, 2003.** Enter as often as you wish, but each entry must be mailed separately. One entry per envelope. Partially completed, illegible, or mechanically reproduced entries will not be accepted. Sponsors are not responsible for lost, late, mutilated, illegible, stolen, postage due, incomplete, or misdirected entries. All entries become the property of Dualstar Entertainment Group, LLC., and will not be returned.

3. Sweepstakes open to all legal residents of the United States (excluding Colorado and Rhode Island), who are between the ages of five and fifteen by April 30, 2003, excluding employees and immediate family members of HarperCollins Publishers, Inc., ("HarperCollins"), Parachute Properties and Parachute Press, Inc., and their respective subsidiaries and affiliates, officers, directors, shareholders, employees, agents, attorneys, and other representatives (individually and collectively "Parachute"), Dualstar Entertainment Group, LLC., and its subsidiaries and affiliates, officers, directors, shareholders, employees, agents, attorneys, and other representatives (individually and collectively "Dualstar"), and their respective parent companies, affiliates, subsidiaries, advertising, promotion and fulfillment agencies, and the persons with whom each of the above are domiciled. Offer void where prohibited or restricted by law.

4. Odds of winning depend on the total number of entries received. Approximately 250,000 sweepstakes announcements published. All prizes will be awarded. Winners will be randomly drawn on or about May 15, 2003, by HarperCollins, whose decisions are final. Potential winner will be notified by mail and will be required to sign and return an affidavit of eligibility and release of liability within 14 days of notification. Prizes won by minors will be awarded to parent or legal guardian who must sign and return all required legal documents. By acceptance of the prize, winner consents to the use of his or her name, photograph, likeness, and personal information by HarperCollins, Parachute, Dualstar, and for publicity purposes without further compensation except where prohibited.

5. One (1) **Grand Prize Winner** wins a Movie Madness Party for the winner and 10 friends which consists of the following: nine (9) videos starring Mary-Kate and Ashley (WHEN IN ROME, GETTING THERE, HOLIDAY IN THE SUN, WINNING LONDON, SCHOOL DANCE PARTY, OUR LIPS ARE SEALED, PASSPORT TO PARIS, BILLBOARD DAD, and SWITCHING GOALS; $250.00 worth of movie passes to a movie theater chain to be chosen by sponsor; food (including popcorn, soda, six foot deli sub sandwich, deli salads). Approximate retail value: $585.00.

6. Only one prize will be awarded per individual, family, or household. Prizes are non-transferable and cannot be sold or redeemed for cash. No cash substitute is available. Any federal, state, or local taxes are the responsibility of the winner. Sponsor may substitute prize of equal or greater retail value, if necessary, due to availability.

7. Additional terms: By participating, entrants agree a) to the official rules and decisions of the judges, which will be final in all respects; and to waive any claim to ambiguity of the official rules and b) to release, discharge, and hold harmless HarperCollins, Parachute, Dualstar, and their affiliates, subsidiaries, and advertising and promotion agencies from and against any and all liability or damages associated with acceptance, use, or misuse of any prize received in this Sweepstakes.

8. Any dispute arising from this Sweepstakes will be determined according to the laws of the State of New York, without reference to its conflict of law principles, and the entrants consent to the personal jurisdiction of the State and Federal courts located in New York County and agree that such courts have exclusive jurisdiction over all such disputes.

9. To obtain the name of the winners, please send your request and a self-addressed stamped envelope (residents of Vermont may omit return postage) to Movie Madness Party Sweepstakes Winners, c/o HarperEntertainment, Attn: Children's Marketing Department, 10 East 53rd Street, New York, NY 10022 by June 1, 2003. Sweepstakes Sponsor: HarperCollins Publishers, Inc.

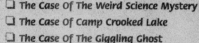

Reading Checklist
andashley

ingle book!

- ❑ Let's Party!
- ❑ Calling All Boys
- ❑ Winner Take All
- ❑ P. S. Wish You Were Here
- ❑ The Cool Club
- ❑ War of the Wardrobes
- ❑ Bye-Bye Boyfriend
- ❑ It's Snow Problem
- ❑ Likes Me, Likes Me Not
- ❑ Shore Thing
- ❑ Two for the Road
- ❑ Surprise, Surprise!
- ❑ Sealed With A Kiss
- ❑ Now You See Him, Now You Don't
- ❑ April Fools' Rules!
- ❑ Island Girls
- ❑ Surf, Sand, and Secrets
- ❑ Closer Than Ever
- ❑ The Perfect Gift
- ❑ The Facts About Flirting

so little time

- ❑ How to Train a Boy
- ❑ Instant Boyfriend
- ❑ Too Good To Be True
- ❑ Just Between Us
- ❑ Tell Me About It
- ❑ Secret Crush
- ❑ Girl Talk

Mary-Kate and Ashley Sweet 16

- ❑ Never Been Kissed
- ❑ Wishes and Dreams
- ❑ The Perfect Summer
- ❑ Getting There
- ❑ Starring You and Me
- ❑ My Best Friend's Boyfriend

MARY-KATE AND ASHLEY in ACTION!

- ❑ Makeup Shake-up
- ❑ The Dream Team
- ❑ Fubble Bubble Trouble
- ❑ Operation Evaporation

Super Specials:

- ❑ My Mary-Kate & Ashley Diary
- ❑ Our Story
- ❑ Passport to Paris Scrapbook
- ❑ Be My Valentine

Available wherever books are sold, or call 1-800-331-3761 to order.

Books created and produced by Parachute Publishing, LLC, in cooperation with Dualstar Publications, a division of Dualstar Entertainment Group, LLC. TWO OF A KIND TM & © 2003 Warner Bros. THE NEW ADVENTURES OF MARY-KATE & ASHLEY TM & © 2003 Dualstar Entertainment Group, LLC, MARY-KATE AND ASHLEY SWEET 16, MARY-KATE & ASHLEY STARRING IN, SO LITTLE TIME and MARY-KATE AND ASHLEY in ACTION! © 2003 Dualstar Entertainment Group, LLC. America Online, AOL, and the Triangle design are registered trademarks of America Online, Inc.

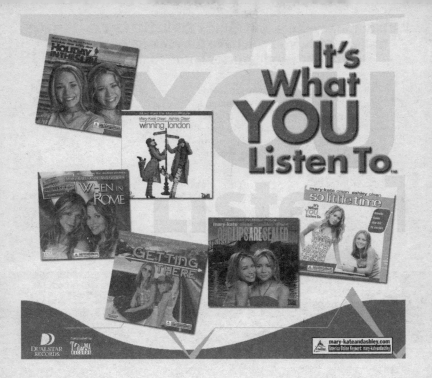

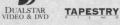 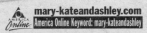

With our Mary–Kate and Ashley so little time fashion dolls, you can have fun making our hit ABC Family series come to life.

I play Chloe and I'm taking a painting class. You can help me finish this portrait with real paints.
–Ashley

I play Riley and I'm taking a photography class. You can help me develop fun photos.
–Mary-Kate

DUALSTAR CONSUMER PRODUCTS

mary–kateandashley

America Online

mary-kateandashley.com
America Online Keyword: mary-kateandashley

MATTEL

AMERICA Online

mary-kateandashley.com
America Online Keyword: mary-kateandashley

DUALSTAR VIDEO